PRAIRIE

STORIES, ARTICLES, & PHOTOGRAPHS

BY SANDRA GRACE

Sandra Fram

AUTHOR & EDITOR
Sandra Grace

WEBSITE
WINGSINTHESTORM.CA

PHOTOS
HOME FOR THE NIGHT BY PAULI KRUGER

STOCK PHOTOS
PRICELESS TREASURE (WATERMARK); OUT OF MANY WATERS; THE BEST OF CHILDHOOD; A HAYFIELD ON AN AUGUST NIGHT

ALL OTHER PHOTOS
Sandra Grace

PRAIRIE

Prairie

by
SANDRA GRACE

I pull to the side of the road and grab my camera. Before me stretches a gorgeous plain in August colors that begs to be immortalized. I stand just off the highway, feeling the heat of the day, hearing the flick of grasshoppers in the long, dry grass. I snap one picture after another, pleased with what's showing on my viewscreen. This new-found interest in photography has awakened me to the beauty of the vast, vibrant prairie.

If anyone thinks southern Saskatchewan is sepia, flat, or boring, that person must never have seen it in summer. So much of its expanse is smooth, rolling hills covered with velvet colors that change almost daily. Deer and antelope roam its plains, and above, red-tailed hawks play on the wind. Prairie dogs stand at the side of the road, watching all who pass, their tiny hands clasped in front of them like mischievous little choir boys, feigning innocence.

There are gravel back roads that run for miles with acres and acres of farmland and grainfields. There are fences and cattle; dust from combines at work; fields dotted with bales of hay; little ponds, shrubs, and tumbleweed. The terrain, ever changing, is the same. It whispers of quiet summer days that lull the spirit and restore the soul.

There's something interesting about the prairie. Just as it hypnotizes into expectancy of its safe, peaceful flow, over the next hill, the earth is suddenly cut away, exposing rough, sharp walls of layered rock. The long, flat plain, ripped open, plunges deep to a vast desert floor. Scrub brush, grasses, sage, and dirt stretch across the bottom of the canyon. A lazy creek winds through, splitting the valley with a flash of brilliant blue.

Such rugged majesty commands attention; such lonely grandeur takes one's breath away.

For all the charm of the soft, flowing prairie, the deep gorges and rough stone sometimes make the most striking landscapes.

Sometimes it's God's ripping open and cutting away that fashion the things most beautiful.

For all the charm of the soft, flowing prairie,
the deep gorges and rough stone sometimes make
the most striking landscapes.

Castle Butte - Big Muddy Badlands SK
Sandra Grace Photography

Big Muddy Badlands SK
Sandra Grace Photography

Priceless Treasure

Rare and bright and beautiful... Of infinite worth... It doesn't happen often and can catch you by surprise—that exceptional someone who enters your life and makes an inexplicable connection... That one who "gets" you like nobody else does—your best friend; your kindred spirit. Souls knit together.

She holds you up when you're weak, cheers you on when you need encouragement, cries with you through your sorrows, applauds you when you embark on new adventures, and celebrates with you in your victories.

She lets you be yourself. You can talk about anything. You don't have to guard your words; she won't use them against you. She doesn't just agree with everything you say, though, so you can believe her when she commends you.

When everybody else thinks you're weird and a little scary, she accepts you and all your crazy with open arms and patient smile.

Her wonderfully wacky sense of humor keeps you giggling. When things are rough, she pulls out her comedy, and the two of you laugh like fools together.

When your load is too heavy, she carries it with you. At your lowest, she's there, listening. She lets you vent and cry and pour out your heart even though you're not thinking straight, and your words come out all wrong. Her response: "I know." That's it. Nothing more. She doesn't lecture you. No reprimand; no advice. She doesn't tell you what you need to do or how you should think or feel. She knows you'll clean up your mess and sort it all out when you're strong enough. She'll keep her eye on you, though. She'll gently warn you if you slip into resentment, and she'll prod you if your anger lingers. But for now, she allows you the sweet release you need. She's been there, too.

And when it's her turn to falter, she looks to you, knowing you've got her.

She's your support; your encouragement; your accountability; your sounding board; your laughter; your sister.

A priceless treasure.

by Sandra Grace

OUT OF MANY WATERS

by Sandra Grace

Hunted by the king...on the run from the royal army, he's escaped time after time. He's fled one wilderness for another, hiding in caverns while those sent to kill him pass by outside.

David stands now at the narrow opening of his refuge, just short of where the early sun touches the dirt floor. In his hand, he holds a scrap of cloth cut from the king's garment. It was only this morning that he'd emerged from the dark shadows and crept up on his enemy, undetected, right here in this very cave—close enough to touch him; close enough to kill him. Yet, David had spared the king's life. *I will not stretch out my hand against the Lord's anointed*—a decision that will cost him, for the enemy will keep coming.

David doesn't know it yet, but it will be years of running...years of loneliness and of fearing for his life. His best friend will be killed in battle. In David's absence, his young wife will be taken and given to another man. He'll be betrayed by those he loves. Forsaken. Rejected. At times, he'll despair.

Moment by moment, David doesn't see God rush to intervene; he doesn't know how it will end. Still, through every adversity, God is with him, directing the events that will

shape his future. Jehovah never forgets His own.

Long afterward, when his enemy is dead and David is king in his place, David pens a beautiful Psalm about God's deliverance. From his private alcove in the palace or maybe sitting on a green hillside at dusk, the former shepherd boy unfolds a magnificent description of his Lord's rescue:

> *"The Lord is my rock and my fortress and my deliverer, My God, my rock, in whom I take refuge... In my distress, I called upon the LORD... He heard my voice...*
>
> *"Then the earth shook and quaked; and the foundations of the mountains were trembling and were shaken because He was angry. Smoke went up out of His nostrils, and fire from His mouth devoured... He bowed the heavens also, and came down with thick darkness under His feet... He sped upon the wings of the wind... The Lord also thundered in the heavens... He took me; He drew me out of many waters. He delivered me from my strong enemy... He rescued me... For I have kept the ways of the Lord..."*
> (Psalm 18, ESV)

Hearing David's cry, God moves. The depth of God's love for His child in physical danger is wondrous. He unleashes His anger against David's enemies, clashing; erupting; spewing; turning nature inside out. He tears through the heavens to rescue His own, as if nothing else matters at this moment but gathering His child safe into His arms.

David's metaphor in this Psalm illustrates a staggering truth. How incredible that the Creator of the universe would be so affected by the plight of one small man. How humbling that a holy God would delight in him who is broken and fallen.

David recognizes the reason for God's help is, first, because of his trust in the future sacrifice of the coming Christ and, second, because of his consistent obedience to God.

For those who've trusted Christ, the God of David's shelter and deliverance is our God, too. His love for us is just as real; just as deep; just as strong. No matter what sorrows He allows us to endure, whether or not He chooses to rescue us from difficulty in this life—and He may not—He is still with us and always cares for us.

One day, He'll rescue us from all enemies; all heartache; all suffering; all sin. He'll draw us out of the troubled waters of this world and gather us to Himself where we will be forever safe with Him.

1 Sam 23:14. 1 Samuel 24: 4–7. Deuteronomy 31:6 & 8. Hebrews 13:5 & 6. Philippians 4:13. Romans 10:9 & 10. Ephesians 2:8 & 9.

The Best of Childhood

STOCK PHOTO

There's an old farmhouse down a winding road. I can see it plainly—white with green gables, just like in the story of Anne. Past the house runs a dirt driveway that splits at the elm tree and goes all the way back to the tin-covered barn.

To the right of the house is an orchard of old, twisted apple trees that are perfect for climbing. There are lilacs and blossoms, fragrant in spring. Surrounding the house is an ample yard—cherishing, protecting—where childhood unfolds in its warm embrace. Beyond the yard are vast, green fields that reach to forever, and thick forests of mystery entice us to wander.

We're two little girls in pigtails and ponytails, bare feet and denim, with lace on our sleeves. Through endless days of soft summer breezes, we explore our paradise together. Stepping through hayfields and sweet-smelling clover, gathering bouquets of daisies. Riding through woodlands of sundrops and shadows, galloping, spirited, innocent, hopeful, free as the wind.

Far back in the field, hidden from view, is a grove of maples—haunting...intriguing. It's guarded by a thicket and brimming with wildflowers, and its cool depths call us to come and explore. Two little adventurers, without hesitation, go into the heart of a wonderland. We find heroes and villains and fairy tale castles in this secret hideaway, our Promised Land.

Swimsuits and sneakers...hot summer days... We skip down the road with our dog at our side. Over the gate and through a pasture to rambling brook of frigid water, sparkling in the light. Splashing; swimming; lots of laughter. Then shivering, dripping, we warm up in the sun. Dragonflies; butterflies; skippers; minnows; peaceful satisfaction. They're long afternoons of simple pleasures and daydreams by pools in our Garden of Eden.

Afternoon sunshine, and we're off catching frogs at the pond down Gillespie Lane. With muddy faces and hair in tangles, we're sloshing and darting after our prize, lost in a world without time. Then come the kisses of raindrops, and dark clouds threaten. With the rumble of thunder, we're hurrying home. Flashes of lightning on blackening skies, and we dance in the downpour, carefree in the storm.

There's an old farmhouse down a winding road. I can hear it plainly, calling me back to sunny days and dusty lanes, to gardens of make-believe and little girl dreams. Ice castles; bicycles; fairy dust trails; sneakers and hairbands; daisy tiaras. Come back with me, Sister, to those hayfields at sunset, to the brook and the forests, the ponds and the flowers and songs on the wind.

Canola Fields by Sandra Grace

July on the prairies is my favorite month. The colors are stunning as gardens and fields burst into bloom. Here in southern Saskatchewan, long, blue sky stretches out over low, rolling hills that are carpeted in velvet hues: green, yellow, purple, and rust. Canola fields, in quiet brilliance, extend to the horizon. The view is endless. If you've not seen it, now is the time. You'll never forget the colors of a Saskatchewan summer.

In the Red Deer area of Alberta, the landscape is more varied: the hills are taller, and there are more trees. The Rockies are to the west, and the foothills offer breathtaking vistas. Alberta has countless intriguing places to explore, and I've motorbiked over much of the southern part of that province.

Even the canola takes on a different personality in Alberta. From atop a hill, you can see for miles: farms, forests, fields, sparkling blue ponds, countless shades of green. It's always a striking view, but particularly when the canola's in bloom. It's like a giant can of paint tipped over, and thick, bright yellow spilt down the emerald slopes, pouring between the woods and the ridges and the ponds. Sassy and playful.

The cacti that grow in our deserts, our prairies and Badlands, the muskeg, cliffs and gorges, endless skies, and mountain peaks... I never knew the wonders of this great country of Canada...

Until I came to see them for myself.

Ordinary

by Sandra Grace

I used to think life was ordinary. Every day, the same. It surrounded me and all that I knew—the schedule, the places, forests, fields, and skies; snow and rain. It had all been there since as far back as I could remember, and it was still there. The same, every day.

There's nothing wrong with ordinary. It's security. Smooth and calm. Easy.

Boring.

And sometimes it can make you feel like you're missing out.

But how did I look at those things without seeing them? How did I not recognize them for what they were? What if ordinary isn't boring after all? What if it holds within its depths all that you've been looking for?

I'm not sure what brought about the change for me or even when. Eleven years ago, I left the lush, green Maritimes for the soft, rolling prairie and its yellow wheat fields. Things were a bit tough; money was tight. My yearning for travel to exotic lands had to be squelched; it just wasn't possible anymore.

I began to explore the places right on my doorstep. Slowly, I started to see what had been in front of me all along.

"The smell of the woods is so soothing," my hiking companion commented one day as we walked a trail in an Airdrie park. I breathed it in, savoring the damp fragrance of moss and earth... hearing the chitter of chipmunks and the snap of twigs underfoot.

It was soothing. The minute I'd stepped into the trees, I'd felt my whole being relax. The welcoming hug of the forest I knew well. I'd missed the woods. I hadn't even realized what a privilege it had been to grow up with them as my playground.

How lovely they were—common old trees. I watched their playful leaves flutter in the breeze while sunlight filtered through their branches and danced on the forest floor.

So beautiful, these ordinary things.

I started to see the world in color. The same stars shone brighter. Spring blossoms smelled sweeter. The same moon went from trivial to captivating—a golden disc as it rose, then silver at its height, different every hour of the night and changing with every phase.

There's the way the silence of a midnight snowfall envelops the soul like the quiet presence of a trusted friend. The glitter of the hoar frost in the morning light... How the fields wave at the touch of a breeze and shimmer in the setting sun...

It's all been here, waiting for me to notice.

The beautiful ordinary. Marvelous and intoxicating.

Not boring at all.

"The heavens declare the glory of God..."
Psalm 19:1

Great Sand Hills
Sandra Grace Photography

Sandra Grace Photography

Big Muddy, SK
Sandra Grace Photography

Prairie Snapshots

by Sandra Grace

Lone
Prairie—
Fragrant fields,
Unending skies,
Painted morning light...

Lilies and wild roses;
Rocky bluffs and desert sage;
Brush of amber, mauve, yellow bright.

Songs of the plains, melodious and sweet—
Sweep of eagle's wings; rustling stands of wheat;
Screech of falcon soaring high above the earth;
August winds, heartless, scorch the sunbaked dirt;
Crash of thunder, savage in the night.

Sunset kisses the horizon;
Slanted rays caress the fields,
Gleaming gold, russet, white...

Twilight rests the land;
Living, Healing,
Ever mine—
Prairie,
Home.

HAYFIELD ON AN AUGUST NIGHT

Stock Photo

Even now, one whiff of freshly cut hay, fragrant and sweet, and I'm back in that field across from our house on an August evening. I'm ten years old, heading home to get ready for bed, the first one to be dismissed from the work.

It's cooling off, the air is damp, and the sun is starting toward the horizon. Crickets chirp—the song that means the end of the day and rest and home. I walk through a haze of dust that seems alive in the fading light. Little insects hover just above the field, and bugs jump through the sharp stubble left after the cut. I'm terribly scared of anything that creeps or crawls, but out here, it's okay. The pleasure in everything else around me on these magical evenings cancels out my fears.

On these nights, my job, most often, is to drive the old Massey Ferguson. I try not to jolt as I work the levers and let out the clutch. My father tells me I'm doing a good job, but it's hard to get the speed just right. I do my best to keep a nice steady pace while the men pick up the bales and load them onto the wagon that I tow behind me.

When it's my turn on the ground, I struggle to lift the bales, they're so heavy. I tug and grunt.

The twine digs into my hands. The men tell me I'm strong, but I can't throw the hay the way they can.

When I've had enough of the heavy work, I climb up onto the wagon—my favorite part. Those on the ground toss the bales to the men up here who pack them in tightly, making sure the load is balanced.

I perch on a ledge several tiers up and survey the field, my hand raised to shade my eyes. A hundred yards off, I can see my dog, her tail wagging in furious delight; she sniffs at the ground, darting after mice that scurry for new shelter now that the crop is cut.

The wagon sways on the bumpy field. Someone calls to me to get out of the way, and I dart to the other side while they fill in the spot I just left. I watch the stack grow, the blocks fit together like a jigsaw puzzle.

The tractor and wagon are behind me now. The men are throwing on the last few bales before calling it quits. I trek home alone—dirt in my hair...sweat on my neck...itchy arms and legs. The slanted evening sun kisses my face. A familiar warmth fills me, though I don't know where it comes from. I'm happy and satisfied. All is right and good in the world at the close of another summer's day.

by Sandra Grace

THE WOODLAND'S KISS

by Sandra Grace

We walked the familiar trail just as we had a dozen times before. It was one of our favorites and well worth the hour's drive. It wound through the woods, out along the edge of a meadow, and back into the forest on the other side. There were offshoot trails, many of which we'd explored already. Each one held its own allure, like a waterfall or a spreading tree that offered its canopy for shade and rest.

Today, we took the longest trail; the prettiest. Hundreds of prairie roses smiled at us from either side. They waved in the summer breeze as though pleased to see us here together again. We went hand-in-hand, sometimes laughing; sometimes in silence, just soaking in each other's nearness.

The hours flew by until we rounded the last turn and faced the rough and cragged hill we knew well. "You up for the climb?" he asked me.

"We have to. Today of all days," I told him.

We took the steep footpath upward, sometimes skidding on loose gravel and reaching for each other to steady ourselves. We grabbed hold of gnarled roots and protruding rocks to pull ourselves up and over the places where the ridge jutted out above our heads.

Then abruptly the trail levelled off. We left the path and picked our way through a mess of brush until we came to the ruins of an old stone wall, set at the edge of a bluff. We climbed the fallen blocks and hoisted ourselves up onto the highest part of the wall. There, our view was unhindered, and the scene beneath us was always spectacular, no matter the day or the season. That's what made this our favorite spot of all the trails we'd discovered together.

Today, the valley below was alive with color. There were verdant forests, bright yellow canola, powder-mauve flax, and a blue-green river that shone like a jewel. There were farmers in the fields and a horse-drawn carriage moving noiselessly along a dusty road. We stood, soaking it in — the vibrant hues; the smell of summer heat and sunbaked dirt and fresh-cut fields. It was almost enough to make us forget the real world. If only we could stay right here and not go back...

He took my hand, and we sat on the wall, our legs dangling down over the side. We stayed for a long time, and we talked of many things — the last of the things we needed to say. The late afternoon light slowly turned the yellow patchwork below us to gold; and when we'd said all that was in us, we put those matters away. We made our way down the rugged hill one last time. Our long walk back felt heavy. Neither of us wanted it to end.

"Hey sweetheart, look at this," he called softly as he reached the clearing just before the parking lot. I came up beside him, and he slipped his arm across my shoulders. I followed his gaze, up and all around us. The setting sun glinted through the trees; it played with the fluttering leaves. Its light caught the downy poplar fluffs that floated on the air. I hadn't noticed them until that moment. The little

tufts danced and glittered — tiny gold pinpoints like fireflies, they rose and fell at the caresses of the breeze. "Like a thousand shimmering dreams," he whispered.

For those few moments, everything else stopped: our problems went out of existence, our differences were mended, and our paths would endlessly be intertwined.

But this enchanted garden would never yield a fairy-tale ending; not for us. For after this walk tonight, we would each begin a new direction, apart from one another. The magic that flitted around us — touching us, teasing us — was not a celebration of happily ever after but a kiss to send us on our way. The gentle breath of summer was a farewell song, and the sparkles on the poplar fluff were tears to see us go.

We would gather it all up and carry it with us to pull out over and over in the days to come...to remember what once was... to see and hear and feel it again... The last performance by the woodland we so loved.

The last dance; the last song; the last goodbye.

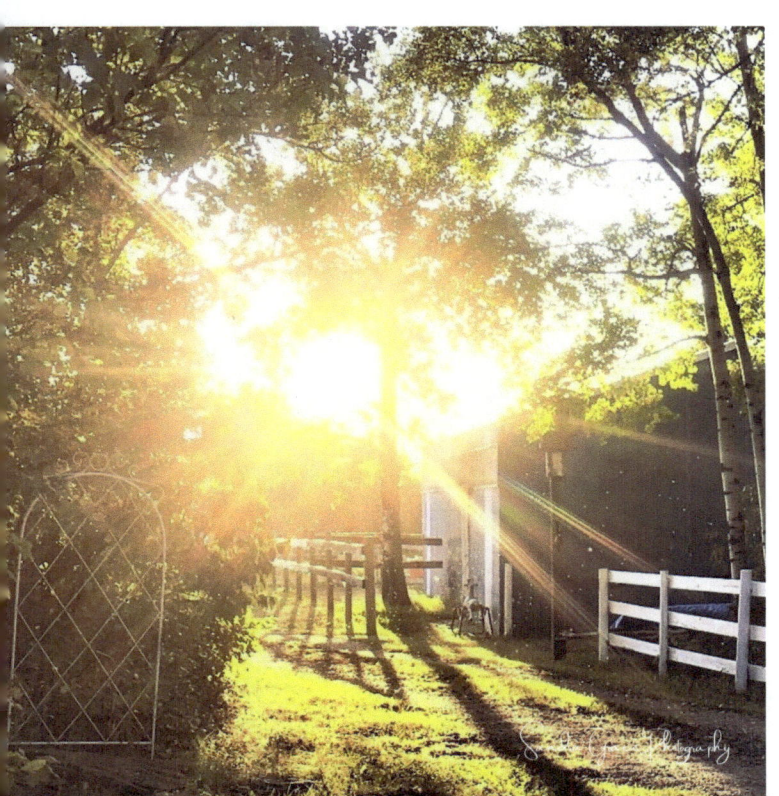

Prairie Gems

There's beauty in the aged,
In the faded and scarred,
Those battered by changing seasons
And weathered by winds of time.

Through empty window frames and broken walls
Come whispers of yesterday—
Echoes of laughter and
The delighted squeals of children;
Farewell kisses in the morning and
Soft good nights on summer twilight breezes.

Ancient gems of the prairie,
Staunch against an ever-changing world;
They bear the marks of a purpose fulfilled,
A testament, not to perfection,
But to faithful endurance,
Steadfast; willing; strong.

by Sandra Grace

Home for the Night

MY BREATH CATCHES. I'M RIVETED, AN UNSEEN INTRUDER, WITNESS TO THIS SPECTACULAR DISPLAY.

Tonight, I'm waiting for it. Watching.

The sun slowly makes its way toward the horizon. Deep blue sky stretches downward and merges into pink, then orange where it touches the hilltops to the west. Reflections shimmer on the waters below my balcony. The warm air stills with expectation.

Then I hear them calling. It's faint at first, they're so far off. I search the sky and soon locate tiny specks to the west, moving through the blue. As they approach, I can make out the sweep of their wings, carrying them on the air, light and sure...

Canada geese.

They begin to take shape: long, sleek necks;

plump bodies; slender black heads; blazes of white. Another flock appears from across the sky, calling to the first, announcing its arrival. It's the beginning of a ritual that will go on for the next hour.

Arcing toward the water, the geese begin their descent. I know their pattern, yet it's new every time. Suddenly, they break formation. They duck and swirl, darting opposite directions and back again, circling each other; down, then up—a spontaneous dance, mid-air. They move as though unaware of each other, yet the whole performance is an intricate choreography, timed to perfection. Playful. Elegant.

My breath catches. I'm riveted, an unseen intruder, witness to this spectacular display.

THE RACKET ON THE POND FADES TO RESIGNED BABBLING. A SLIGHT CHILL BRUSHES MY SKIN. I SLIP AWAY NOW.

Then, their recital ended, they drift downward, gliding on the soft breeze. With a flutter of wings, they touch the surface, skimming across the water in effortless grace. Magnificent.

And skein after skein, they arrive home as darkness deepens. The last of them come in droves as though they are late. They hurry in to join the others. There are two or three hundred, now, in all. They settle in groups all over the pond, honking, fretting, squawking. The night is filled with their noise, and I know why they are called a gaggle.

Above them, the sliver of white moon glows brighter, reflected on the water. Moments pass, and a tinge of yellow seeps across the white. The stain slowly darkens as the deep blue sky around it turns velvet black. The moon edges downward. At last, it glows orange just before it's gone.

The racket on the pond fades to resigned babbling. A slight chill brushes my skin. I slip away now.

Their clucking will go on all night. I sink into the melody, lulled by the rhythm. My geese are home, guided back by the One who gathers the scattered and brings order out of chaos.

We tuck into His hands.
The night folds in around us.
Peace. Rest. Home.

by Sandra Grace

Matthew 6:26. "Look at the birds of the air: they neither sow nor reap nor gather into barns, and yet your heavenly Father feeds them. Are you not of more value than they?" (ESV)

My geese coming home
Airdrie, AB
Photo by Pauli Kruger

Airdrie, AB
Photo by Pauli Kruger

Photo by Pauli Kruger

SANDRA GRACE

Sandra Grace was born and raised in Moncton, New Brunswick. She moved to the Saskatchewan prairies in 2012 and later relocated to Alberta.

She discovered her love of photography around her pond in Airdrie, AB ("Home for the Night") and through her many explorations of Alberta and Saskatchewan. She started with just an old cell phone and admits that everything she knows is the result of trial and error.

In 2020, Sandra spent two months in Costa Rica working on her memoir, *Wings in the Storm: Hope & Healing through Brokenness*, published in 2021. She's the author of four children's books under the name, Sandra Fram.

Sandra lives in Shaunavon, Saskatchewan. She works as an administrator; is the co-editor of an online monthly magazine; and enjoys motorbiking, hiking, photography, travel, family & friends, and of course, writing.

BOOKS

Wings in the Storm; Hope & Healing through Brokenness

Prairie Blossoms Winter

CHILDREN'S BOOKS

The Secrets of Amethyst Cove

Runaway Teeth

Happy Birthday, Mrs. Gimbal

Priscilla's Leaves
    co-authored with her daughter, Grace

CONTACT HER
sgracewrites@outlook.com

WEBSITE
wingsinthestorm.ca

"The Woodland's Kiss" is fiction.

All other stories and articles in *Prairie* are taken from real events.